MG KIDS

Real Super Heroes Eat Fruits and Veggies

Coloring book
By
Charles Lovjoy

ISBN:978-1-7373302-9-5

MUSCLE GANG PUBLICATIONS

MG KIDS

Other books from

MG KIDS

MG KIDS

Please leave a review on Amazon and follow us on facebook.com/mgkids.charles

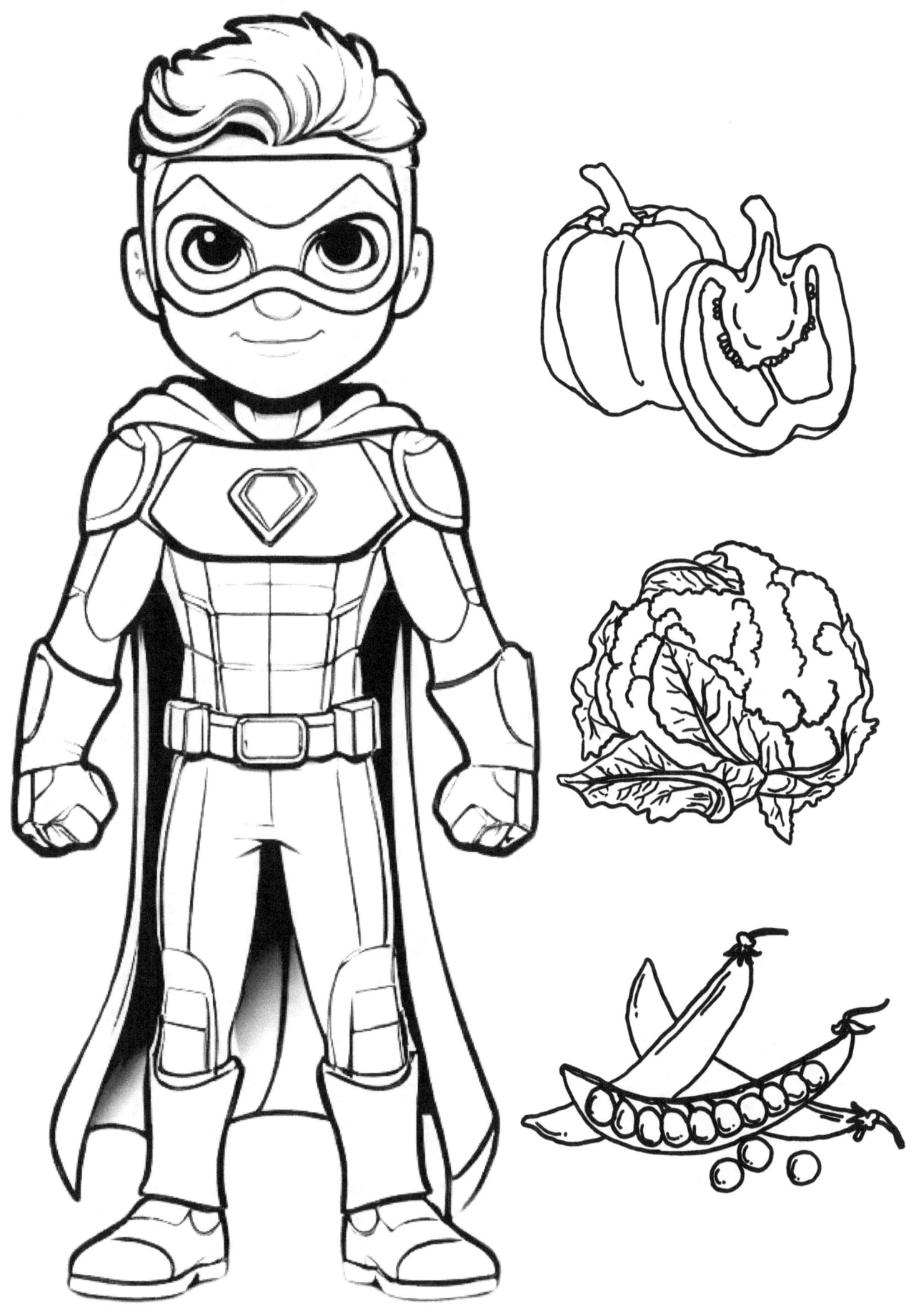

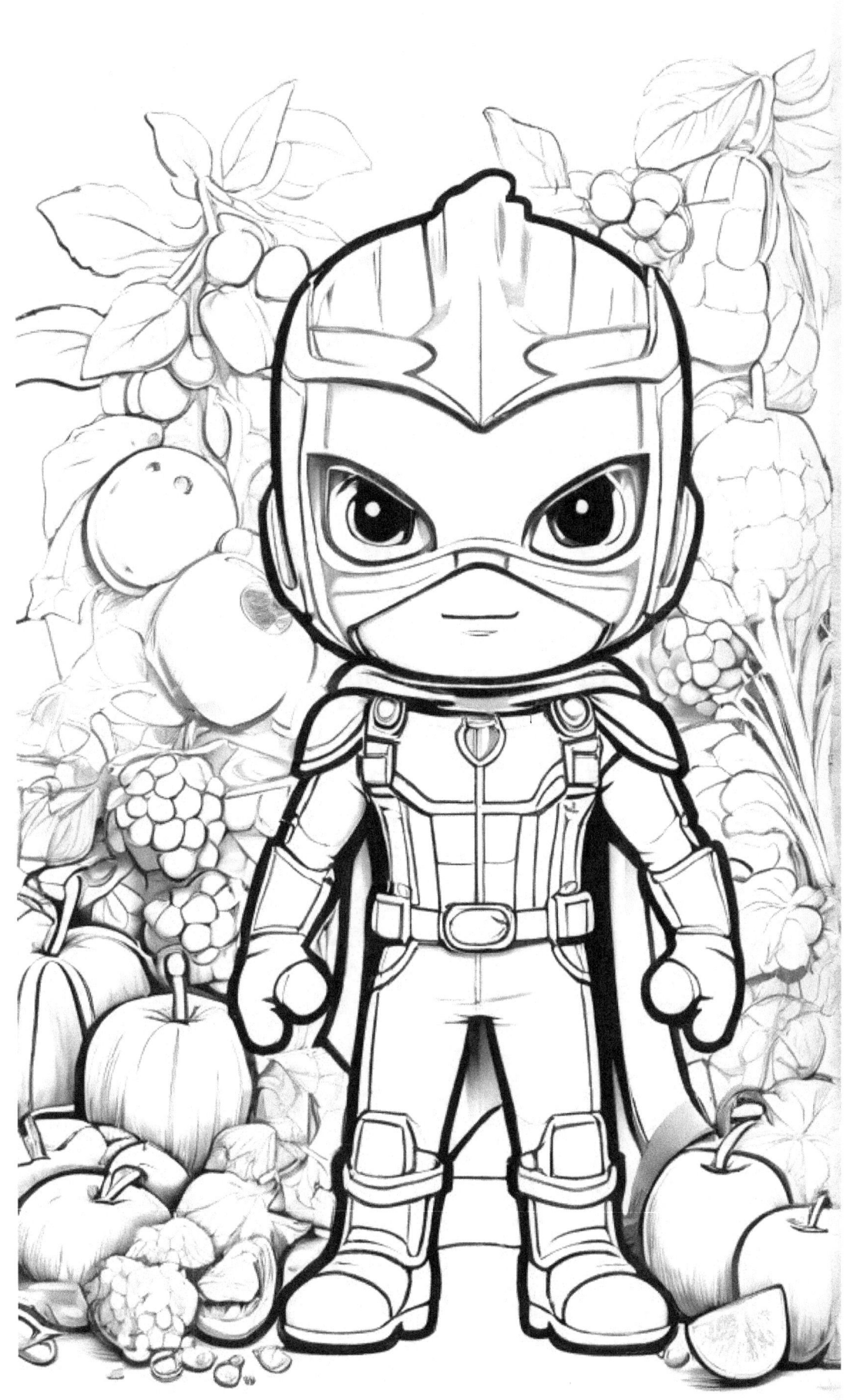

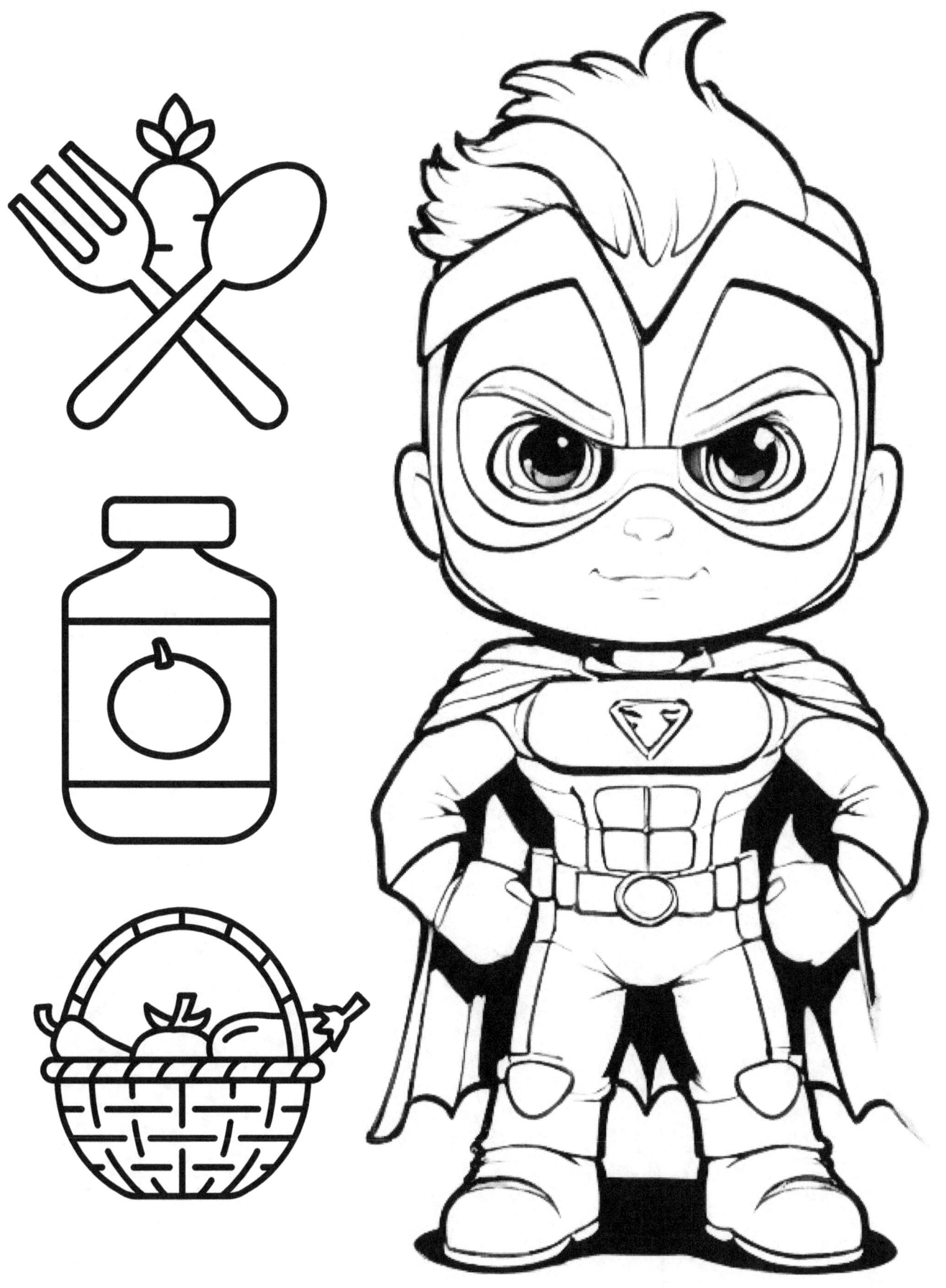

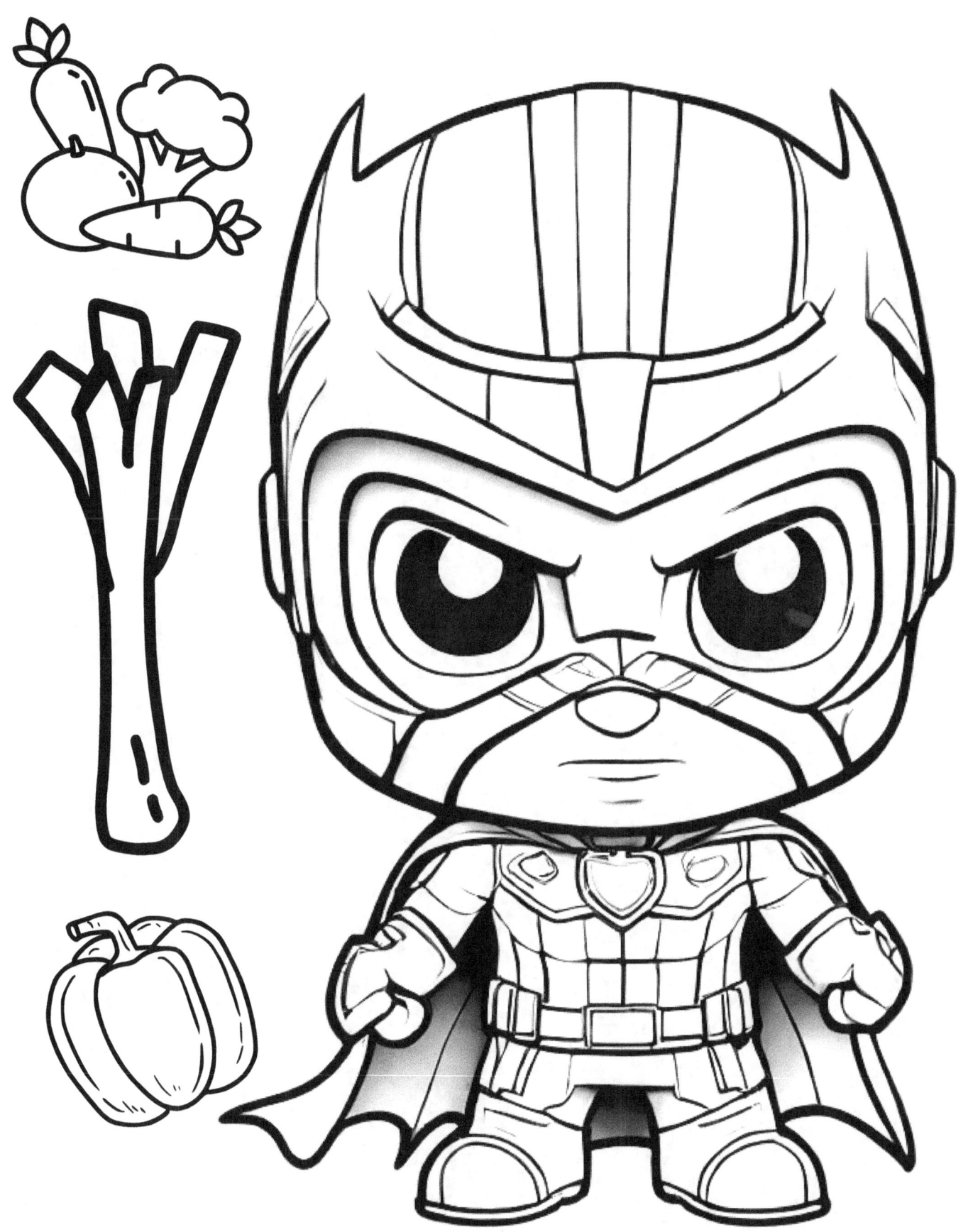

www.ingramcontent.com/pod-product-compliance
Lightning Source LLC
Chambersburg PA
CBHW080753120626
46557CB00005B/1253